Satanic Bedtime Stories

Written by Christy Leigh Stewart

Illustrations by Megan Hansen

Published by
Good Mourning Publishing
Manteca, California, USA

http://goodmourningpublishing.com/

Published October, 2012

All works in *Satanic Bedtime Stories* are works of fiction. Names, characters, places, and incidents are the products of the author's imagination or are used fictitiously. Any resemblance to actual events, locales, or persons, living or dead, is entirely coincidental.

ISBN: 0615710492
ISBN-13: 978-0615710495

This book intends to be a usable teaching tool for parents wanting to raise their children with Satanic values.

The Nine Satanic Statements were authored by Anton Lavey as standards of conduct for the members of the Church of Satan who maintains their copyright to this day and are as follows:

1. Satan represents indulgence instead of abstinence!

2. Satan represents vital existence instead of spiritual pipe dreams!

3. Satan represents undefiled wisdom instead of hypocritical self-deceit!

4. Satan represents kindness to those who deserve it instead of love wasted on ingrates!

5. Satan represents vengeance instead of turning the other cheek!

6. Satan represents responsibility to the responsible instead of concern for psychic vampires!

7. Satan represents man as just another animal, sometimes better, more often worse than those that walk on all-fours, who, because of his "divine spiritual and intellectual development," has become the most vicious animal of all!

8. Satan represents all of the so-called sins, as they all lead to physical, mental, or emotional gratification!

9. Satan has been the best friend the Church has ever had, as He has kept it in business all these years!

Satan represents indulgence instead of abstinence!

Damien, a bright eyed and curiously minded young boy, was delighted when he was invited to stay with his cousin for the weekend. The two of them always had a wonderful time whenever they were together, each excelling in creating a greater adventure than the other.

As soon as the weekend began, the boys decided to take Damien's cousin's action figures outside and have them battle. It was an exciting battle, but after not too long Damien's aunt came and told them they had to take a break. Damien thought she was going to give them a snack, like his mom does when he's playing at home, but instead his aunt had them sit quietly at the kitchen table. Damien asked her why he and his cousin couldn't keep playing. She told him that it was bad to have too much fun, and abstinence makes them better people.

When dinner was served Damien was hungry, not having had a snack, and everything smelled so good that he wanted to gulp it all down like a seagull would a fish, but remembered what his mom had taught him about table manners, and so he ate slowly. Right before he had almost eaten everything on the plate his aunt took it away and put it in the sink. Damien asked her why he couldn't finish diner. She told him that it was bad to be full, and abstinence makes them better people. Even though

Damien was still hungry, he didn't say anything and joined his cousin to play a board game in the living room.

They were having a good time and Damien was sure he was going to win, but right before they were done, Damien's aunt made them put it away. Damien asked her why they couldn't finish the game. She told Damien too much winning would make him bad, and abstinence would make him a better person.

Damien was beginning to feel frustrated and felt even worse when his aunt announced it was almost time for bed, but she let them watch some TV first. They watched a cartoon with gritty pirates and beautiful sea creatures, but before their adventure was over, Damien's aunt turned the TV off. Damien asked why she turned off the TV. She told him watching too much TV would make him bad, and abstinence would make him a better person.

For the first time in his life, Damien was happy to go to bed but even sleeping too much was bad, according to his aunt. She woke him and his cousin periodically through the night, saying too much sleep would make him bad, and abstinence would make him a better person.

When the weekend had ended and Damien returned home, he was sleepy, hungry and in a terrible mood. He didn't feel like a better person at all; he just felt unhappy.

Damien asked his mother why abstinence hadn't made him better or happy. She told him that sometimes people who are scared of life keep themselves from being too full of food, or fun, or love. They believe that if they lack something that they become stronger, but in fact, it makes them weaker. She said Damien should eat until he was full, work until the job was complete, play until the game was over, rest until he was refreshed and love as much as his heart could bare.

Satan represents vital existence instead of spiritual pipe dreams!

Fang was a beautiful and majestic wolf cub who lived in the exotic forest with his pack, along with all kinds of plants, animals and insects. The only creatures that Fang knew of that he hadn't grown up among were the birds.

They never came down to the forest floor, and Fang couldn't jump as high as the tree tops. No matter how loud he howled up to them, they never answered him, they just continued to sing to each other. Fang's pack told him to ignore them, but it was hard to do when they were always gliding through the trees and singing while Fang had to hunt and help take care of the den. It seemed like the birds didn't have a care in the world, and Fang was constantly working.

One afternoon, while Fang was stalking a rabbit for dinner a little red bird flew over head, distracting him so much that he almost lost the rabbit, but remembering his training and empty stomach, he quickly sniffed out his prey again. He crouched down on his agile limbs, about to pounce on his dinner, when the little red bird swooped down again with a loud SQUAWK that sent Fang stumbling into a tree and the rabbit escaped into it, s hole.

"What did you do that for?" Fang demanded.

"You should have seen your face!" the bird chirped. "You were so serious and then POOF you failed. Don't take things so seriously!"

"That was my dinner," Fang told the bird, "If I don't

catch something I'll go to bed hungry."

"That's silly. You won' t go hungry if you believe in the Holy Wobble; he'll always provide food for his worshipers."

"Who is the Holy Wobble?" Fang asked.

"He is a god that lives higher than the tree tops, higher than the clouds, higher than the stars. As long as we believe in him, he wont let anything bad happen to us. That's the problem with you wolves. You work and work trying to find more food, more water, better homes. Just tell the Holy Wobble that he is your god and he will provide for you."

Could that be true? Is that why the birds had such great lives? They never had to work because the Holy Wobble provided everything they needed? He would protect them as long as they believed in him?

"I believe in you Holy Wobble!" Fang howled into the sky. "Please bring me some dinner!"

Fang waited all night and nothing happened, so he went to bed hungry.

The next day, the little red bird found him hunting again. "What are you wasting your time hunting for?" he asked.

"I'm starving because the Holy Wobble didn't bring me dinner!" Fang growled.

"That's because you have to sing to him, tell him how great he is."

Fang was frustrated. He was tired and hungry and didn't know if he could trust the bird again. "How can I tell the Holy Wobble how great is he if he lives so far away he can't even hear me?" Fang asked. "How do you even know about him?"

"The other birds taught me about him and they told me he can hear everything, everywhere. The monkeys believe in him too, as do the sloths. You never see them worrying, do you? The monkeys are constantly playing and the sloths sleep all the time."

That was true... "Okay," Fang gave in, "I'll sing."

So Fang sang all day long, praising the Holy Wobble. He sang about how kind and wise and beautiful the Holy Wobble was, even though he had no idea if it was true.

That night, Fang went to bed hungry.

The next day, the little red bird came to mock Fang's hunting again.

"Why are you still working for food?" the bird asked.

"Because The Holy Wobble didn't bring me any dinner! I sang all day long!"

"Oh, you can't just believe in him and sing to him, you have to get other animals to do those things too. Spread the word of The Holy Wobble."

There were so many rules, it seemed like nothing Fang did was enough. He wanted to give up, but he thought of how easy life would be if he never had to work or hunt again, and so he turned tail and went back to his pack to tell everyone about The Holy Wobble.

"Where did you hear about this?" Fang's mother asked.

"A little red bird. He said that the birds and the monkeys and the sloths didn't have to work because they believed in The Holy Wobble."

"Those animals have to work just as much as we do!" his mother told him. "They build dens and nests, just like us. They gather fruit like we hunt. You can't survive on belief of a higher power, you have to be constructive and work!"

Fang went out to hunt again and this time he

ignored the little red bird. Fang caught his prey and was finally full. Once his belly was full and he could finally relax, Fang watched the tree tops and saw the birds, even the little red one, gathering their diner.

"Why are you working so hard?" He called up to the little red bird.

The little red bird ignored him and kept working so he wouldn't starve.

Satan represents undefiled wisdom instead of hypocritical self-deceit!

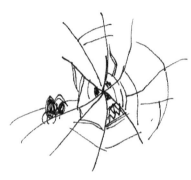

Lilith was a beautiful spider, as spiders go, but very average in most ways. She was neither the first nor the last of her siblings to hatch from their mother's egg sac; her antennae were neither long nor short. When it was time to make her first web, it was nothing if not average.

Her siblings, on the other hand, competed amongst each other to create the most artistic and ornate webs possible. They created webs that sparkled like jewels when the morning dew settled on them, and they created webs that were charactertures of other creatures such as the neighborhood dog and a woman who tried to kill them with cans that blew out poisonous smoke.

"Lilith has no talent," one of her brothers said.

"Lilith is not an artist," added another.

Despite their taunts and how hurtful to her their words were, Lilith said nothing. Her webs may not be as beautiful as her siblings' but they were strong and efficient, they worked perfectly to trap the flies and small insects that kept her well fed and so she was happy.

The artistic competition escalated and the webs became more ornate; so much so that the spiders stayed up days working on the new webs, never stopping to feed themselves and even becoming angry when their prey became caught and ruined the design they had worked so hard on.

"Is it so important to have the most beautiful web when creating it leaves you starving?" Lilith asked.

"It is you who will starve," said a sister that had become thin and weak. "Y. Our webs are so plain, no creature will come near them. Soon we will all be well fed on the bodies of those creatures who appreciate our art. Wait and see!"

No amount of pleading or reasoning seem to get through to Lilith's siblings, and one by one they worked themselves to death and Lilith was alone – well fed and happy but lonely and surrounded by beautiful webs that hung empty and useless.

Satan represents kindness to those who deserve it instead of love wasted on ingrates!

There was a celebration in the forest.

On the longest night each year, when everything was cold and dark, the animals of the forest came together in peace and ate a great feast. Fang, being a young wolf cub, had only joined in on the celebration the year before, but now he was old enough to pitch in and help his elders prepare.

For a week, the forest was abuzz with excitement for the coming festivities, even though everyone was working hard to hunt and forage enough to feed every animal that was attending. Fang worked hard to do his part and make his pack proud of what he could contribute. As the wolves were leaders, they were in charge of most things, and so they had to make the greatest effort for the celebration.

Coming back from one tiring day of preparations, Fang was halted by the sound of soft crying. He looked high and low to find it, but he hadn't searched low enough, for it was coming from a tiny ant beside his paws.

"Why are you crying?" Fang asked the little ant.

"I want to go to the long night celebration," said the little ant.

"Then come!"

"Insects aren't allowed to go," the tiny creature told him sadly.

Fang didn't remember seeing any of the insects taking part of the celebration before and he had never wondered why, but now he felt very badly and extended an invitation to the ant. "You and your colony may come, the only rule is that you must bring something to eat for the celebration. I see you collecting leaves and such. I don't eat those myself, but some of the other animals do."

"Thank you!" cheered the small ant.

Fang was overcome with happiness when he returned to the pack and headed straight for his father to tell him about the conversation he had had with the ant.

"There is a reason the insects aren't invited to our celebration," Fang's father told him patiently. "They only take care of their own kind and have never brought anything to the celebrations for anyone but themselves. That is not what the long night is about."

"I told the little ant he must bring food for the other animals when he and his colony come," Fang told him.

"If the ant colony follows the rules and brings food to share then they are allowed to come. We'll welcome any creature."

Fang was sure that the ants would bring food with them on the longest night, but when the celebration finally began and the ants arrived, they had nothing with them.

"I told you to bring food," Fang told the little ant who had cried, worried that his father would be angry at him for the ant's mistake.

"I told my colony and they said they would only bring food for our Queen and no one else. They said they have seen you all working hard so there should be enough food anyway."

This made Fang a little angry because he remembered what his father said about the rules and what the long night was about. "This is a night where we set aside our differences and give freely to one another out of love," Fang told him, "you can't expect to enjoy everyone's love and hard work without giving anything in return."

"We ants don't feel like we should give to anyone but ourselves."

Fang shook his head sadly. "Then you won't receive anything from anyone else."

Fang left the ant he had thought would become his friend and returned to the celebration. He was sad that the ants hadn't followed the rules and couldn't enjoy the festivities, but he also felt more proud of the other animals who had done their part. They were true friends, and Fang would happily work hard to help them any time he could.

Satan represents vengeance instead of turning the other cheek!

As a spider Lilith was not inclined to venture out into the world. She was born within the eave of a beautiful home in a sunny neighborhood, and she made her nest in the tree in the yard; lifeless, peaceful and uninterrupted until an owl moved into her tree.

At first, Lilith was more than happy to share her tree with the owl. There was more than enough room for the both of them and whereas she depended on smaller insects to feed herself, the owl had her fair share of mice to keep her well fed, but before long Lilith found the webs were being destroyed each time the owl flew through them.

"Would you mind trying to avoid my webs?" Lilith asked the owl.

"I could simply eat you and there wouldn't be any more webs for me to fly through," taunted the owl.

The threat scared Lilith and she didn't respond; she simply remade her web and tried to avoid the owl.

She remade it again and again, each time feeling more and more terrified of the owl and her disregard for Lilith's life and livelihood until Lilith became too hungry and realized that she would starve to death unless she did something, so why should she be scared if the owl ate her?

Lilith waited until the owl had left her nest and quickly set up on it, covering it in thick, sticky strands of her web and then waited for the owl to return. When she did, the owls claws became stuck in the web and while she struggled to get free Lilith spun around her to entrap her wings to her side with even more web.

"Why are you doing this?" pleaded the owl.

"Now you understand what it feels like to be scared and helpless; now you know what you have done to me and if you can get yourself free you will think twice before doing it again."

Lilith left the owl trapped in her nest, and although she eventually got free, she left Lilith and her webs alone.

Satan represents responsibility to the responsible instead of concern for psychic vampires!

Summer had come and with it a long awaited vacation from school for Damien. He was excited to have time to play with his friends every day in bright skies and cool pools. His mother set aside a day each week for play dates with friend's two children. One was a boy named Scott, and the other was Eric.

At first, Damien wasn't too excited to go over to a stranger's house to play with someone he didn't know. He would have rather spent time with other children he knew, playing games he already knew, but after the first day with the other boys, he found he enjoyed it a lot. With his new friends came new games, new jokes, new toys, new snacks. Damien found himself looking forward to his play dates each week.

Scott was the youngest brother; he liked video games and collected comic books. Eric was only a little older than Damien himself; he liked playing sports in the back yard and was always the one who asked their mother when they were going to eat. Each boy was a lot of fun to play with, and even though they never agreed on what game to play, they never really fought either. Because of their differences, they often played separately, and Damien had to play with them one at a time.

Scott was really good at his video games and would teach Damien all of his tricks until he was just as good and they could win the games together. When they talked, they talked about school and friends and family. Scott was a good listener and was always interested in what Damien had to say. Whenever something funny or bad happened to Damien, Scott was the first person Damien thought of; he couldn't wait to talk to him about it.

Eric wasn't as patient as Scott was. When they would play games in the backyard, Eric wouldn't explain all the rules until Damien had broken one. If he didn't win enough, Eric would become angry and insist that Damien go play with Scott again. Eric and Damien talked as well, but most of the time Eric would do most of the talking. If Damien began a story, Eric would interrupt him to tell his own. If Damien had a problem, Eric would tell him that his life was worse. If Damien got hurt, Eric would tell him about a time when he was twice as hurt.

Eventually, Damien didn't want to spend as much time with Eric. He would feel tired even thinking about him. It felt like the only reason Eric wanted Damien around was to complain to him. He didn't want to see Eric anymore, but how would he be able to see Scott without seeing Eric?

Damien explained the situation to his mother and asked what he should do.

"Eric is a psychic vampire," His mother explained, "Psychic vampires are people who need other people's energy to survive; they have close friends they call donors who will give them their body's energy a little bit at a time to survive. Sometimes, though, psychic vampires will make you feel sad or mad so they can take the energy you create from it without you knowing. Regular humans do the same thing sometimes – using other people's feelings to make them powerful. Eric is this type of person."

"What should I do?" Damien asked, not wanting to be a victim of this kind of vampire.

"You should never have anything to do with people who just want to use you," Damien's mother explained. "You should only have respect for people who treat you as well as you treat them. Just like real psychic vampires will give their donors energy back and sometimes heal them when they are sick, you want a friend who will give you attention back and make you feel good."

Damien's mother told him that she would have Scott come over to their house for play dates, and he didn't have to play with Eric again unless he wanted. Damien began feeling happy again and was never tired when he heard Eric's name.

Satan represents man as just another animal, sometimes better, more often worse than those that walk on all-fours, who, because of his "divine spiritual and intellectual development," has become the most vicious animal of all!

Fang, the wolf, lived deep in the forest with his family pack, never knowing any life beyond his own. He and his pack lived a peaceful and prosperous life, and so Fang never thought of leaving his home until one day when his older brother told him that humans were nearby; never having seen one before, Fang suggested that they go see them, but his brother said no. He said that it wasn't safe, but Fang ignored his warnings and snuck off to find them anyway.

At first he heard them, their grunts and howls indecipherable to Fang. Their sounds were so loud and brave that Fang imagined them as giant beasts that could crush him under their heel, but the humans looked a lot like the monkeys that swung from the trees only less hairy, slightly taller, and a lot funnier looking in general.

They had other animals with them as well, ones Fang had seen many times but also some he had never seen before. The animals all had their own den's that were square and surrounded by tree limbs that sparkled like water; the humans called them cages.

The life of these animals with the human's looked great! Their cages were warm with grass but still open enough to see the forest;. They were fed meats already rendered from the bone without having to hunt. They were brought water to their own beds. This seemed like a much better life than the one Fang was living. He had to share his space with all of his family members. He had to hunt and fish and find water. He had to build his own bed.

It was an easy decision Fang made to make his new home with the humans and exotic animals. He slowly approached a human in greeting as not to startle them but before he could even say hello one threw a bag over his head and drug him into a cage of his own.

Despite the rough initiation into their pack, Fang was happy to see his clean bed, fresh meat, and cool water bowl.

"What are you so happy about?" asked a large and colorful cat in the cage beside his own.

"I get to live like you now!" Fang told him. "I never have to work, the humans will take care of me and I will always have a bed."

The cat scoffed. "You are confused, my friend; your new life isn't a good one. The humans will never let you out of your cage and you will never have the joy of running free or seeing your family again. You will have to do tricks for the humans or they will beat you and not feed you. Look at some of the fur they wear. They didn't grow it from their bodies; they took it from other animals!"

Fang was shocked and terrified he had made a terrible mistake. "Why would the humans do this to their fellow animals?" he asked.

"The humans believe they are smarter than us, and because they believe in a god that looks like them, they think that they are allowed to do anything they wish to other creatures. As a wolf, other animals fear you just as they feared me for being a tiger, and so we hunt and eat , them, but we only take as much as we need where, as the humans will kill us for the fun of it," the cat explained.

"Is there no way for us to escape or convince the humans to let us go?"

"There is no hope for us, wolf."

Fang still did not give up. Every time a human walked by he begged to be let go and when he was alone he would howl for his family.

No one answered, and no one ever came.

Satan represents all of the so-called sins, as they all lead to physical, mental, or emotional gratification!

The woman that lived inside of the home overlooked by Lilith's tree was strange; sometimes she was quiet and would sit with a book and other times was frantic and would jump around to music so loud that it would make limbs of Lilith's tree shutter. Lilith could never anticipate what the woman would do and that made her all the more fascinating, so one day Lilith snuck into the house through an open window to get a closer look.

Although the woman was much larger in person, she was less entertaining than she appeared from the window. She ate, she rested, she cared for her children; all things that Lilith was familiar with and so it bored her.

"Why don't you dance? Why are you singing? I traveled a long way from my tree, I want to do something fun with you!" Lilith told the woman but the woman could hear and couldn't understand.

"I don't mean to intrude; I thought we could be friends." Lilith climbed the wall until she could become visible to the woman but once she was, there was no time for introductions.

The woman screamed and threw her shoe, crushing Lilith to death.

The woman didn't know that Lilith was friendly and did not intend to hurt her.

The woman was scared of the way Lilith looked and him and him and him and him and of the stories that she had heard about poisonous spiders that could make her body bloat and ooze.

The woman's preconceived notions kept her from making a good friend and resulted in her killing an innocent creature.

Satan has been the best friend the Church has ever had, as He has kept it in business all these years!

Damien had a quiet boy in his class named Adam. He never saw Adam talk or play with anyone because none of the other children liked him, although he seemed nice to Damien. A popular boy in class, David, told the children at the beginning of the year not to talk to him; none of them did. Not even Damien, although he had no reason to dislike Adam.

David told the children that Adam had cooties, and lice, and bad breath.

David told them that Adam was stupid, and mean, and said bad things about them.

David told them that Adam wanted to get all of them in trouble and keep them from their real friends.

He never talked to Adam, and so Damien never got to ask him if it was true. Pretty soon, the other children were saying the same things as David. It didn't seem mean, because they were trying to protect themselves from Adam. If they befriended him they would also become gross, and mean, and trouble makers.

The more they hated Adam, the closer all of the kids became. They would play together once a week on the weekend and sing songs, play games, and remind each other to do the right thing so we wouldn't become like

Adam.

Damien and the children were all very happy until one day Adam's family moved away.

Damien thought things would be better because now he didn't have to worry about what Adam would do or say to the children, or if one of them would turn on the others to be his friend. A lot of them were looking forward to the rest of the year, but soon things got bad.

David told the children that their friend Sarah was now worse than Adam had been. She was more smelly, cursed, stole from the teacher.

Other kids were blaming Robin or Anthony, Peggy, and Lue.

Everyone turned against each other and none of them were friends anymore.

Without someone to blame everything on, they didn't know who hate and didn't know how to trust each other if there was no one around to blame all the trouble on. They became scared of their friends and worried if they were right about the horrible things they were saying about them, even if they made them up.

Adam had been their best friend; because they could blame everything on him, they could always be popular.

Satanic Bedtime Stories

Satanic Bedtime Stories

Satanic Bedtime Stories

Satanic Bedtime Stories

Printed in Great Britain
by Amazon

60236988R00020